DATE DUE			
NOV	MAR 22		
DEC 11	DEC 21		
JAN 15			
APR 1	MAR 0		
MAY 23			
OCT 29	NOV 02 NOV 23		
FEB 18	DEC 08		
FEB 25	JAN 07		
MAR 09	JAN 14		
MAR 17	NOV 11		
APR 1	JAN 1 1		
APR 15	OCT 0 5		
OCT 01	FEB 0 5		
NOV 09	APR 1 9		
NOV 24	SEP 0 2		
DEC 01	MAR 1 0		
DEC 07			
DEC 10			

Desert Critter Friends

DESERT DETECTIVES

Mona Gansberg Hodgson
Illustrated by Chris Sharp

SAINT LOUIS

Dedicated to Carolyn, Melissa, Katherine, Summer, Julie, and Jamie—some of the kindest kids and young adults I know.

Desert Critter Friends Series

Friendly Differences   *Campout Capers*

Thorny Treasures   *Sticky Statues*

Sour Snacks   *Goofy Glasses*

Smelly Tales   *Crabby Critters*

Clubhouse Surprises   *Spelling Bees*

Desert Detectives

Jumping Jokers

Scripture quotations taken from the HOLY BIBLE, NEW INTERNATIONAL VERSION®. NIV®. Copyright © 1973, 1978, 1984 by International Bible Society. Used by permission of Zondervan Publishing House. All rights reserved.

Copyright © 1999 Mona Gansberg Hodgson

Published by Concordia Publishing House
3558 S. Jefferson Avenue, St. Louis, MO 63118-3968
Manufactured in the United States of America

Library of Congress Cataloging-in-Publication Data

Hodgson, Mona Gansberg, 1954–
    Desert detectives / Mona Gansberg Hodgson ; Illustrated by Chris Sharp.
        p.   cm. — (Desert critter friends series ; bk 6)
        Summary: Myra discovers an animal sleeping in the Desert Critter Clubhouse and she and her animal friends learn that it is a ringtail who was separated from her brother by a fire on their mountain home.
    ISBN 0-570-05083-9
    [1. Ringtail—Fiction. 2. Desert animals—Fiction. 3. Helpfulness—Fiction. 4. Christian life—Fiction.] I. Sharp, Chris, 1954-   ill.
II. Title.   III. Series: Hodgson, Mona Gansberg, 1954-   Desert critter friends ; bk. 6.
PZ7.H6649De   1999
[E]—dc21   98-34391
                                                              AC

2 3 4 5 6 7 8 9 10   08 07 06 05 04 03 02 01 00

Myra, the quail, stepped out of
her nest. *Whoosh!* The wind blew a
twig over her top-knot. *Boom!*
Thunder roared. Lightning zigzag-
ged across the cloudy sky.

Myra marched along the path.
She was on her way to tidy up the
Desert Critter Clubhouse for her
friends.

A strange smell tickled Myra's
nose. *Sniff. Sniff. Sniff.* Just then she

saw smoke on Mingus Mountain.
She hoped the fire wasn't hurting
any of her friends.

Myra scurried inside the cave
that she and her friends had made
into a clubhouse.

"Zzzzz!"

It sounded like a snore. Myra looked around. She didn't see anyone.

"*Zzzzz!*" The snore was louder. She wasn't alone! Myra looked around again and spotted the rock pile.

Myra fluttered to the top of the rocks. She peeked down between them. She saw a big fluffy black-and-white-striped tail. It looked like Rosie, the skunk.

Myra fluttered down from the rock pile. She didn't want to wake Rosie. Myra stacked games and books. She dusted the table.

"*Achoo!*" Someone sneezed. Would Rosie sneeze in her sleep?

"*Achoo!*" Just then Rosie dashed through the doorway and into the clubhouse.

"Rosie?" Myra scurried over to the skunk. "I thought you were already here."

"Hi, Myra. The wind tried to blow my bow away!" Rosie straightened her hair bow. "Looks like you're cleaning. I'll help you."

"*Zzzzz!*"

"That isn't you sleeping over there?" Myra pointed to the rocks.

"I don't snore!" Rosie whispered.

"But it has a stripe like yours. Come look." Myra marched up the rock pile. Rosie climbed behind her. They looked down at the mystery visitor.

"That's not a skunk,"
Rosie whispered. "The stripes
go the wrong way."

Myra took another peek at
their visitor. She stepped back to
look at Rosie's tail. "You're right,"
Myra whispered. "Your stripes are in
a line. Those stripes are in a ring."

Zoom! Bert, the roadrunner, zoomed into the clubhouse. "It's raining hard out there." He took his backpack off. "What's that?" he asked.

"*Shhh.*" Myra put her wing up to her beak. "A mystery visitor is sleeping in the rocks." She pointed down into the rock pile.

"*Zzzzz!*"

Bert took off his backpack.
"It's not a critter we know?"

"We don't know what it is,"
Rosie whispered. She stepped back
and put her paw over her mouth.
"*Achoo.*"

"It has a stripe on its tail, but it'
not like Rosie's," Myra whispered.

"Zzzzz!"

Bert zoomed up on the rocks
and peeked at the visitor. He told
Myra and Rosie to follow him. He
zoomed down off the rocks. Myra
fluttered off the rocks. Rosie
climbed down behind her.

"It doesn't have stripes on its back," Bert whispered. "It has seven or eight rings on its tail." He paced back and forth.

"*Zzzzz!*"

"It could be a raccoon," Rosie said.

"Yes, it could be a raccoon." Bert stopped pacing.

"Do raccoons have striped rings on their tails?" Myra asked.

"Yes, but aren't they brown
and black?" Rosie whispered to Bert.

"That's right," Bert said.
"Brown and black, not black and
white. Our visitor has black and
white rings on its tail."

"Zzzzz!"

Rosie climbed up the rocks again. Myra fluttered up behind her. They took another peek. The mystery visitor had stretched out.

"It has white rings around its eyes," Myra reported in a whisper.

Bert paced again. "It's not a raccoon then. Raccoons have black masks on their faces." He zoomed up the rock pile again.

"Hello!" Taylor, the tortoise, called. "It's sure wet out there." He wiped his feet on the rug. "What are you looking at?"

"*Shhh*," the other three friends whispered.

Bert zoomed down to Taylor. "Am-I-glad-to-see-you." It sounded like one word.

"You even whisper fast," Taylor whispered.

"*Zzzzz!*"

Rosie climbed down the rocks to Taylor. "There's a mystery critter sleeping in here."

"What does it look like?" Taylor asked.

"Kind of like a raccoon," Myra whispered. "But it isn't a raccoon."

"I can help you solve the mystery." Taylor strolled over to his bookshelf. "I'll look in my book."

22

"Is it smaller or larger than a raccoon?" Taylor turned pages. "I feel like a detective," he said.

"What's a *de-tick-live*?" Rosie asked.

"A *de-tec-tive*, not a *deticklive*." Taylor chuckled. "A detective is someone who figures out mysteries. My book helps me do that."

Myra whispered, "I'm a detective today. I found the sleeping visitor. Then I figured out that it wasn't Rosie."

"Bert and I are detectives too," Rosie said. "We figured out that it isn't a raccoon."

"It's smaller than a raccoon," Bert said. "It has white rings around its long, bushy tail."

"And white rings around its eyes," Myra whispered.

"*Zzzzz!*"

Taylor pushed his glasses up his nose. "Tell me about its ears and nose," he said.

"Big and pointed," Rosie said.

"Its ears or its nose?" Taylor asked.

Rosie chuckled. "Sorry," she whispered. "It has big ears and a pointed nose."

Taylor flipped more pages in his book. He showed a page to Bert and Rosie. "Does it look like this?"

Bert stared at the picture. "A long bushy tail. White rings around the eyes and rings around the tail. Big ears and a pointed nose. A long, skinny body. That's it."

"Your mystery sleepyhead is a ringtail."

"*Zzzzz!*"

Taylor read his book. "Ringtails like climbing rocks. I guess they like to use them for a bed too."

Bert zoomed away from Taylor to study the ringtail. He zoomed right into a bucket. "*Crash!*"

The desert critter friends froze.
They didn't hear any more snoring.

Myra peeked down at the ringtail. "We didn't mean to wake you," she said. "Bert was zooming and—"

"Wh-where am I?" the ringtail asked. A tear ran down her fuzzy face.

"In our critter clubhouse. My name is Myra. What's yours?"

"Nikki."

"Don't be afraid, Nikki," Myra whispered. "Come meet my desert critter friends."

Nikki crept out of the hole. She followed Myra down the rock pile.

The ringtail sniffed. "Where is Mingus?"

"Mingus Mountain?" Rosie asked. "Is that where you live?"

Bert zoomed over to Nikki. "There's a fire on Mingus Mountain. Is that why you hid here?"

"Don't be afraid." Myra gently patted Nikki's head. "We will help you."

"Where is my brother, Mingus?"

Bert scratched his head. "Your brother's name is Mingus?"

"His name is Mingus, just like the mountain where we live," Nikki said. "Lightning hit a bush. It started a fire. I ran away as fast as I could. I got so tired."

"You must be hungry." Myra marched over to the food bin. She pulled out a cactus apple and handed it to Nikki.

A tear ran down Nikki's face. "I feel too sad to eat. Mingus was by the bush. What if the fire—"

"Don't worry!" Bert said. "I'll be right back." *Zoom!*

"Bert will find your brother," Rosie said. "He runs fast. And we are all desert detectives."

Zoom! Bert was back. He zoomed up to Nikki. "The rain put out the fire."

"Did you see my brother?"

"No, but don't you worry. I'll help you find him."

"I'll go with you," Myra said to the ringtail.

Taylor put his book on the table. "Rosie and I will stay here. Your brother might come looking for you."

"Thanks," Nikki said. "You're all so kind."

"This is where we are." Bert pointed to his map. "This is where the fire was."

Bert poked the map into his backpack. He slipped his backpack on. "Let's go," he said.

"I'll save this." Nikki reached up and put the cactus apple into Bert's backpack. "We might get hungry. First, I want to find Mingus."

"Bye, Rosie." The ringtail
waved to her new desert critter
friends. "Bye, Taylor."

Rosie and Taylor waved back
to her.

"*Achoo!* Bye, Nikki," Rosie said.

"Come back and see us,"
Taylor called.

Zoom! Bert zoomed out of the
clubhouse. Myra and Nikki stepped
out behind him. *Squish! Squish!*
Myra's toes sank into a mud
puddle. She looked around at the
tumbleweeds.

Bert zoomed. Nikki dashed after him. Myra scurried along behind them. The three friends sped around soggy bushes. Bert and Nikki raced to the bottom of Mingus Mountain.

"Hey!" Myra shouted. "Wait for me!"

Screech! Bert put on his brakes. Nikki stopped too.

"M-M-Mingus!" Nikki shouted, just as Myra caught up to them. Myra saw another ringtail waving at them from a rock at the bottom of Mingus Mountain.

"That's my brother!" Nikki jumped up and down. "Thanks for helping me, desert friends." She hurried to greet her brother.

Myra smiled at Bert. "I sure do like it when we can help new friends."

"Me too," Bert said. "Come on. Let's go meet Mingus from Mingus Mountain."

God is your helper! He loves you so much that He sent His Son to pay the price for your sins. That's the best kind of help! You can share God's love by helping others.

Carry each other's burdens.
Galatians 6:2

Hi kids!

Help Myra and me take Nikki to her brother Mingus on Mingus Mountain. Trace the path that leads from the clubhouse to the ringtail on the mountain.

START

WRONG WAY!

For Parents and Teachers:

At times we have all rushed through days filled with the importance of our own agendas, forgetting to offer a helping hand to those around us. We ignore the elderly person struggling with the heavy door at the bank. We may even push our children from one task to another, forgetting their need to be listened to and hugged. We are thankful that Jesus never forgets to help us. His only agenda is that of His heavenly Father's—saving us from sin, death, and Satan. Daily He walks with us, sharing our burdens and helping us with every need.

The desert critter friends were eager to help Nikki find her brother. Kids will take their lead from us. Do they see us running past hurting individuals in order to satisfy shallow agendas? Or do they find us eagerly being used by God to help others?

Remind your children of the little boy who gave his lunch to Jesus. That story about the fishes and loaves is a good example of how God can take the little we have to offer and use it in amazing ways for the benfit of others. Here are some questions and activities you can use as discussion starters to help your children understand these concepts.

Discussion Starters

1. Who did Myra discover in the clubhouse?

2. Why was Nikki, the ringtail, in the clubhouse? What would you do if you found a child who needed help in your clubhouse or in your room?

3. How did the desert detectives learn what kind of animal was sleeping in their clubhouse?

4. What book do we have to help us learn about God's love? Read Hebrews 13:1–3. What do we learn about sharing God's love in those verses?

5. What did the desert critter friends do to help Nikki? What can you do to help someone?

Pray together. Thank God for sending His Son to be your Savior. Thank Him for the people who help take care of you. Ask God to show you how He would have you help others.